PONY PALS

What's Wrong with My Pony?

Jeanne Betancourt

Illustrated by Paul Bachem

A
LITTLE APPLE
PAPERBACK

SCHOLASTIC INC.
New York   Toronto   London   Auckland   Sydney
Mexico City   New Delhi   Hong Kong   Buenos Aires

Thank you to Dr. Kent Kay for his help with this story.

ISBN 0-439-30642-6

12 11 10 9 8 7 6 5 4 3 2 1   1 2 3 4 5 6/0

Printed in the U.S.A.
First Scholastic printing, November 2001

Contents

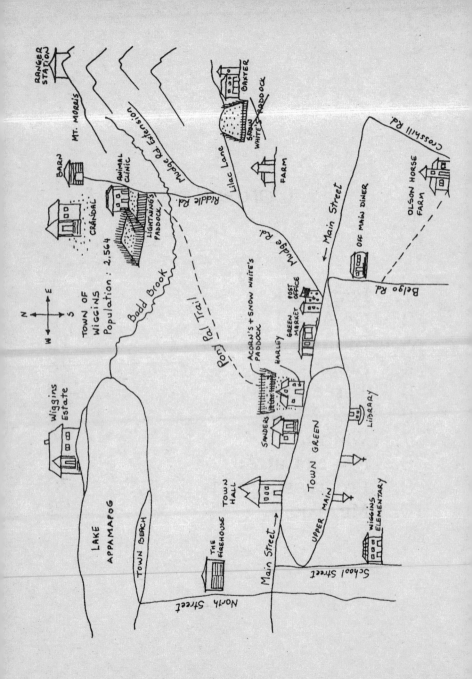

Pony Talk

Pam Crandal looked out the barn window and saw her pony in the paddock. Lightning's chestnut coat shone in the bright morning light. Pam was happy. Today was Saturday and the Pony Pals were going for a long trail ride and picnic.

Pam lifted Lightning's saddle off the sawhorse. It was time to saddle up.

On the way to the paddock, Pam passed the riding ring. Her mother was giving the five-year-old Crandal twins their weekly riding lesson. Pam stopped for a minute at the fence to watch her sister and brother ride. Jack was riding a palomino Shetland pony named Daisy. Jill was *trying* to ride Splash, a feisty Appaloosa pony.

Jill gave Splash the signal to go forward. Splash didn't move.

Mrs. Crandal looked over at Pam. "Splash is being difficult today," Mrs. Crandal told her. "Could you help for a minute?"

Pam hung Lightning's saddle over the fence and walked into the ring. "Give him the signal again," Pam called to her sister.

Jill tapped Splash's side with her heels and said, "Walk on." Instead of going forward, Splash backed up.

"Splash won't do what I tell him," complained Jill.

"I'm afraid he's been spoiled by my beginning students," Mrs. Crandal said. She smiled at Pam. "I know you're going on a trail ride, but could you ride him around the ring a couple of times?"

"Sure," agreed Pam. "Anna and Lulu aren't even here yet."

"Splash needs a firm hand," Mrs. Crandal continued. "I'd do it myself, but I'm too tall to ride ponies."

Pam held Splash while Jill slid off. "Why won't Splash listen to me?" Jill asked.

"Splash can be stubborn," answered Pam.

Jack rode past them. "Daisy's being good for me," he bragged.

"Daisy's an easier pony to ride," Mrs. Crandal reminded Jack.

"Splash will be good for you, too," Pam told Jill. "You have to learn to be firm with him."

Pam mounted Splash and patted his neck. She liked the energetic, strong-willed pony. She could see her own pony in the paddock. Lightning was energetic, too, but she was sweet-tempered. Lightning is the pony I love best, she thought.

"Jack, you ride Daisy in front of Pam and Splash," Mrs. Crandal directed. Jack moved Daisy into position and walked on.

Splash started walking before Pam told

him to. "Whoa," she ordered as she pulled on the reins. Splash kept walking. Pam focused all of her attention on Splash. Okay, Splash, she thought, I'm riding you now. Pay attention to me.

Pam gave Splash the signal to stop again. Splash finally halted.

"Walk on," commanded Pam as she tapped his side with her heels.

Splash moved forward.

She signaled the pony to trot by squeezing her legs.

Splash trotted.

Out of the corner of her eye, Pam saw Anna and Lulu tying their ponies, Acorn and Snow White, to the hitching post. Pam didn't call or wave to her friends. She kept all her attention on Splash.

Splash suddenly rushed to catch up with Daisy. Pam insisted he slow down by pulling on the reins. He did.

Finally, Pam halted Splash in front of Mrs. Crandal and Jill.

Pam dismounted and handed the reins to Jill. "Don't let him get away with *anything*," she told her sister. "Remember to be firm with him."

"Okay," agreed Jill.

Mrs. Crandal smiled at Pam. "Thanks, honey," she said.

Anna and Lulu came into the riding ring. Jack rode over to meet them.

"Pam had to ride Splash for Jill," Jack told Anna and Lulu. "I don't need her to ride Daisy for me."

Anna scratched Daisy's golden mane. "That's because Daisy's such a sweet pony," she said.

"Pam did some good work with Splash," said Mrs. Crandal. "She handled him beautifully."

"Pam's great with ponies," said Lulu.

"She can talk to ponies," added Jill. "She's going to teach me. Right, Pam?"

Pam put an arm around her little sister and gave her a hug. "You have to let Splash know that you care about him *and* that you are in charge."

"That's what I'm going to do," Jill promised.

I do have a special connection with ponies and horses, thought Pam. But my closest pony connection is with Lightning. Her heart filled with love for her pony. She couldn't wait to be on the trails, riding her again.

"Let's go," Pam told Anna and Lulu. "I still have to saddle up Lightning."

The Pony Pals said good-bye to Mrs. Crandal and the twins and headed out of the ring.

Anna pointed at a fluffy gray cat sitting on the hitching post. "Look at Fat Cat," she laughed.

Pam rubbed Fat Cat's soft, furry back. "Fat Cat loves ponies," she said.

"Especially Lightning," commented Lulu.

"She's been lying on Lightning's back a lot," Pam told her friends. "Especially when it's cold."

"That's so cute," commented Anna.

While Anna and Lulu watered their ponies, Pam went to the paddock to saddle up Lightning. "Hey, girl," she called to her pony. "Let's go."

Lightning didn't move. She didn't even look up. Maybe she's asleep, thought Pam. She called again in a louder voice. Lightning slowly walked over to her.

When Pam put the saddle on Lightning's back, the pony scooted sideways. As Pam tightened Lightning's girth, the pony's ears went back. Did I wake her up from a bad dream? Pam wondered as she scratched Lightning's forehead. "Everything is okay," she told her pony. "I'm here."

Anna rode her brown-and-black Shetland pony, Acorn, up to the paddock gate. Lulu followed on her Welsh pony, Snow White. Acorn whinnied hello to Lightning. Pam was surprised that Lightning didn't whinny back.

"We're going trail riding with your pals Acorn and Snow White," Pam told Lightning. "We're going to have fun." She opened the gate and led Lightning out.

"Ready?" Anna asked Pam.

"Let's ride!" answered Pam as she swung up onto Lightning.

When she sat in the saddle, Lightning moved backward. Pam pushed the reins forward. "Whoa," she told her pony. "Wrong direction."

Lulu and Snow White led the way onto Riddle Road. Anna and Acorn followed.

"Walk on," Pam told her pony. Lightning took a few steps forward, then stopped. "Pay attention, Lightning," demanded Pam. "Walk on."

Lightning slowly walked on.

Snow White and Acorn trotted on ahead of them. Meanwhile, Pam shifted her seat and gave Lightning the signal to trot. But her pony stopped again.

What's wrong with Lightning? wondered Pam. Why isn't she paying attention to me?

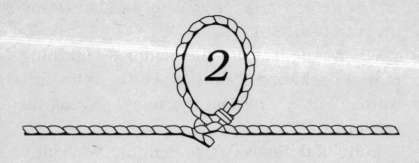

Go Away!

The Pony Pals reached Mudge Road Extension. Anna and Lulu turned their ponies left onto the dirt road. Pam pulled Lightning to the left but the pony didn't want to turn. Lightning snorted and shook her head.

"Go," insisted Pam.

Lightning finally moved forward.

The other ponies picked up the pace again. Maybe I should let Lightning choose her own pace, thought Pam. But when Pam stopped tapping Lightning's sides with her heels, Lightning stopped completely. "Lightning, you're acting like Splash did with Jill," mumbled Pam.

She remembered that Lightning saw her riding Splash. Is Lightning jealous that I rode another pony? she wondered. Pam leaned forward in the saddle and patted Lightning's neck. "The only time I ride another pony is to help my mother," she said. "But I guess you can't understand that."

"Come on, slowpokes," Anna called to Pam and Lightning.

"We're coming," Pam shouted back. She tapped her heels hard against Lightning's side. The reluctant pony walked a little faster.

Pam thought about the first time that she rode Lightning. She knew right away that the chestnut Connemara pony was meant for her. Pam's father was a veterinarian so he checked Lightning's physical condition. Pam's parents agreed that Lightning was a fine pony. That was the happiest day of my life, thought Pam.

Pam knew her Pony Pals felt the same way about their ponies.

Anna Harley began riding lessons when she was five years old. That was the year she met Pam and they became best friends. We were Jill's age then, thought Pam. Mrs. Crandal had taught Anna how to ride on school ponies. Anna didn't have her own pony until she was nine. Everyone agreed that Acorn and Anna were perfect for each other. They were both energetic, lovable, stubborn, and smart. Anna was also a terrific artist. But she was dyslexic, so reading and writing were difficult for her.

Lulu Sanders loved to read, especially books about animals. She learned a lot about animals from her father. Mr. Sanders was a naturalist who traveled all over the world to study animals and their habitats. Lulu's mother died when Lulu was little. After that, Lulu traveled with her dad. When she turned ten, her father said she should live in one place for a while. That's when Lulu moved in with her Grandmother Sanders. At first, Lulu thought Wiggins was boring. But the day she found Snow White and met Anna and Pam, she changed her mind.

Lulu and Anna waited for Pam at a fork in the trail.

"Where are we going to have our picnic?" asked Lulu.

"Let's go to the campers' lean-to," suggested Anna. "It's like a little cabin."

"Okay," agreed Pam.

"What's wrong with Lightning?" asked Lulu. "She's so slow today."

Pam didn't want to tell her friends that Lightning wasn't behaving for her.

"She's warming up," Pam said.

Everyone thinks I'm so great with ponies, she thought. But my own pony isn't behaving for me.

"You lead, Pam," suggested Anna. "You know the way best."

Pam pulled Lightning out in front. She pushed her heels into Lightning's side. "Walk on," she commanded.

Instead of walking, Lightning broke into a gallop. Pam tried to slow her down, but

Lightning kept running. Pam struggled to stay in the saddle and shouted, "Whoa." But Lightning didn't slow down. She finally stopped when they reached the lean-to. Pam regained control and made Lightning walk slowly around in a circle.

Lulu rode up to them. "That trail was too narrow to go so fast," she scolded Pam.

"I know," said Pam.

Anna rode off the trail. "Why did you go so fast?" she asked Pam.

"Lightning ran away with me," Pam said. "She wouldn't slow down."

"You couldn't stop her?!" exclaimed Anna.

"That's not like Lightning," said Lulu.

"I know," said Pam as she dismounted.

Lightning shook her head and snorted as if to say, "I'm glad you're off me."

Lulu dismounted, too. "Couldn't you control her at all?" she asked.

"She wasn't listening to me," admitted Pam. "Right from the beginning of the ride."

"Something must be wrong with her," said Anna as she slid off Acorn.

"We should check her over," added Lulu.

After Anna and Lulu tied their ponies to trees near the lean-to, the three girls gathered around Lightning.

"Maybe her girth is too tight," suggested Lulu.

Pam ran her hand under Lightning's girth. "It's just like always," she said.

"Let's take off her saddle," said Lulu. "Maybe there's a burr under her blanket."

"Or a bee," added Anna.

Pam took off the saddle. There was nothing under the saddle or the saddle blanket that would bother a pony.

Pam took off Lightning's halter and bit. "I'll check her mouth," she said. "Maybe her gums are sore." Pam looked carefully inside Lightning's mouth. "Everything looks normal in here," she reported.

Next, Pam cleaned Lightning's hooves with a hoof pick. The girls carefully inspected the bottom of Lightning's feet. They looked fine, too.

"Maybe Lightning will behave better after a rest," suggested Anna.

Pam tied Lightning to a tree. She gave each pony an apple. Lightning didn't look at Pam when she took the apple. It made Pam feel sad and confused.

The three girls sat facing one another in the lean-to. Pam poured cups of hot chocolate. Lulu passed around peanut butter and jelly sandwiches. Pam didn't feel like eating.

"Why do you think Lightning is misbehaving?" asked Anna.

"Maybe she was spooked by something we didn't see," suggested Lulu. "Like a fox in the woods or a bird flying out of a tree."

"Lightning loves animals and birds," said Pam. "Those things don't spook her." Pam looked down at her uneaten sandwich. "I think she's mad at me."

"Why?" Anna and Lulu asked in unison.

"Because I rode Splash," answered Pam. "She's jealous."

"Maybe she was jealous for a little while," said Anna. "But she wouldn't stay mad."

"She'll be better after a rest," concluded Lulu.

Pam stood up. She wanted to be close to her pony. She wanted to tell Lightning how much she loved her.

"I'll be right back," she said.

Pam went over to Lightning, untied the lead rope, and led her away from the other ponies. She looked into her pony's eyes. Pam thought Lightning looked sad.

"I love you," she told her pony. "I love you more than anything else in the world. Let's be friends again."

Lightning nodded as if she understood. Pam kissed the upside-down heart marking on Lightning's forehead. Then she leaned her weight on Lightning's back to give her a big hug. Suddenly, Lightning snorted angrily and scooted sideways.

Pam fell to the ground with a thud. The sky swirled above her. Lightning's hooves were near her head.

Is Lightning going to trample me? she wondered.

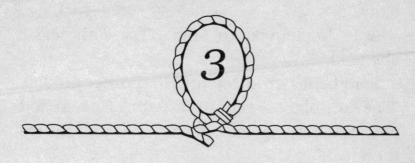

Biting

"Pam, what happened?" shouted Lulu.

Anna leaned over her. "Are you all right?" she asked.

"Lightning," whispered Pam fearfully.

"Lulu has her," said Anna.

"Don't try to get up," shouted Lulu. "I'll be right there."

Pam saw Lulu tying Lightning to a tree. Pam's rear end hurt. She rubbed her upper arm. "I bruised my arm," she told Anna. "It hurts." She held her arms up in the air and moved them around. "But my bones are okay."

Lulu knelt next to Pam. "Try your legs," she said.

Pam bent her knees and flexed her ankles. "They're okay," reported Pam. She rolled onto her side to get up. "My backside hurts the most."

Lulu helped Pam up and Anna brought her water.

"Now walk a little," Lulu told her. "Just to be sure everything is okay."

While Pam walked up and down in the clearing, she looked over at Lightning. Lightning turned away from her. Why did Lightning hurt me? wondered Pam. Why is she being mean to me? I didn't do anything mean to her. She can't be *that* jealous of Splash. Pam suddenly felt angry at her pony.

Anna came up beside her. "You shouldn't ride Lightning back," she told her. "She's acting too weird."

"We'll all lead our ponies home," added Lulu.

Pam shook her head. "I have to ride," she insisted. "I got dumped, now I have to get back on. Lightning and I have to work this out." She looked in Lightning's direction. "I can't let her get away with it."

"But your butt," said Anna. "It will hurt to ride."

"I have to do it!" said Pam angrily. "Don't you understand?"

"Don't be mad at *me*," exclaimed Anna. "I didn't dump you."

Lulu put a hand on Pam's shoulder and the other on Anna's. "Come on, let's go back."

Pam shrugged off Lulu's hand. "You don't have to come with me," Pam told her friends. "You can ride some more. Your ponies are okay."

Pam knew she sounded grumpy. She *was* grumpy. Her backside was sore. Her arm hurt. And she was confused about Lightning.

"We'll ride together," said Lulu quietly.

"Do whatever you want," mumbled Pam as she rubbed her sore arm.

Anna and Lulu packed up the lunch things while Pam saddled up Lightning. She talked to her pony the whole time. "We're a team, Lightning," she said. "I protect you and you work with me." Lightning turned her head away from Pam.

Anna and Lulu led their ponies over to Pam and Lightning.

"You two ready?" Lulu asked cheerfully.

Snow White sniffed Lightning's face. Lightning squealed and pinned back her ears.

Lulu pulled Snow White away from Lightning. "Wow!" she exclaimed. "What was that all about?"

"I don't know," said Pam. "Let's just go. You guys go first."

"We decided you should go first," said Lulu. "In case you have more trouble."

"I don't want to go first," said Pam.

"It's two against one," Anna told Pam. "So you *have* to go first. That's the Pony Pal rule."

"That's for a Pony Pal Problem," said Pam. "This isn't a Pony Pal Problem. It's my problem with Lightning." She glared at her friends. "Lightning might behave better if she's following other ponies. Didn't you even think about that?"

"We were just trying to help," grumbled Anna.

"You can go last if you want," Lulu told Pam.

"And don't wait for me," said Pam. "Just keep going. I'll catch up."

"Wear your Pony Pal whistle," Lulu said, "just in case."

Pam patted her pocket. "I have it," she said.

Lulu and Anna rode back onto the trail. Pam took a deep breath, put her foot in the stirrup, and swung up on Lightning's back. Lightning scooted to the side. Pam sat firmly in the saddle and pulled on the reins. Lightning didn't respond. Pam pulled harder. Finally, Lightning paid attention to her and Pam directed her pony back onto the trail.

Lightning cantered. Then, suddenly, she stopped. Pam still couldn't control her pony.

Her backside hurt more than ever, and she felt angry at Lightning. Her body tensed up. Pam realized that she was a little afraid of her own pony.

Ahead of them, the other riders turned onto Mudge Road Extension. When Pam signaled Lightning to turn, Lightning bucked. Pam fell to the ground, backside first. She screamed out in pain, then scrambled to her feet and grabbed Lightning's reins. Lightning's ears were back, and anger and fear flashed in her eyes. Pam's rear end stung from the fall. But I have to get back on Lightning, she thought. I have to ride her.

Anna and Lulu galloped up to her.

"What happened?" asked Anna in a worried voice.

"We heard you scream," added Lulu.

"She bucked me off," Pam told them.

She carefully walked around to Lightning's left side. She put her foot in the stirrup to mount.

"Pam, don't ride her now," warned Anna. "It's not safe."

"Lead her home," said Lulu. "Then we'll figure out what's wrong."

Pam took her foot out of the stirrup and faced Anna and Lulu. "What's wrong is that she's angry at me," said Pam. "And she won't do what I tell her."

"You fell twice," Lulu reminded her. "It's too dangerous to ride her on the road."

"You *have* to lead her," scolded Anna.

Acorn moved toward Lightning and love-nibbled her neck. Lightning swiftly turned and bit him. Acorn backed off and whinnied angrily. Anna pulled Acorn away from Lightning.

"Lightning!" shouted Pam. "What's wrong with you?"

"Lightning's not just mad at you," said Anna. "She's mad at everybody."

Me, too, thought Pam. I feel mad at everybody.

"You can't ride her," insisted Lulu.

"All right," agreed Pam.

Pam led Lightning out onto Mudge Road Extension. She remembered how hard she pulled on the reins. I was angry with Lightning when I was riding, she thought. Angry and frightened. And Lightning knows it. I communicated all the wrong things to my pony. It's all my fault.

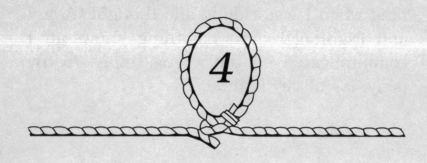

Alone

Half an hour later, the Pony Pals were back at the Crandals'. They took off the saddles and wiped their ponies down. Lightning shook his head angrily when Acorn looked at him.

"Maybe Lightning shouldn't be in the same paddock with Acorn and Snow White," suggested Anna.

"I'm keeping Lightning inside tonight, anyway," said Pam. Her sore arm brushed against the barn door. It hurt. "You can put

28

Acorn and Snow White wherever you want," she added in a grumpy voice.

"Pam, you should tell your mother what happened with Lightning," suggested Lulu.

"Maybe she could ride her and figure out what's wrong," added Anna.

"My mother is too tall to ride Lightning," said Pam sharply. She rubbed her sore arm. "Lightning is my responsibility. I know her best."

Lulu turned away from Pam. "Let's put our ponies in the paddock, Anna," she said.

Lulu and Anna led their ponies outside. Pam thought Lightning would want to follow her friends. But she didn't even look at them.

As Pam led Lightning to her stall, she worried about her pony. She scratched Lightning's upside-down heart marking. Lightning sighed.

"You've had a hard day, too," Pam said as she picked up the towel. "I'll give you a good rubdown and put a blanket on your back."

Pam rubbed the hair on Lightning's side in a big sweeping motion. Lightning suddenly raised her hind leg and struck out. As Pam jumped away from the kick, her bruised backside hit the wall of the stall.

Tears of pain and frustration filled her eyes. Lightning had tried to kick her. She'd never, ever done that before. Pam kept a fearful eye on Lightning while she put out oats, hay, and fresh water. What awful thing would her pony do next?

Pam's tears turned to sobs, but Lightning didn't pay any attention. Pam remembered another time she'd cried in front of Lightning. It was after Grandmother Crandal had died. Pam had cried when she told Lightning. Lightning had whinnied softly and licked away Pam's tears with her soft tongue.

Now Lightning ignored Pam's tears.

Pam looked up to see Lulu and Anna at the stall door.

"Pam, we're sorry we argued with you," said Lulu.

"Friends?" asked Anna with a small smile.

31

"Of course we're friends," said Pam. "I'm sorry, too." She wiped her tears with her sleeve. "I'm not crying because of our fight. I'm crying about Lightning."

"We know," said Anna and Lulu in unison.

Pam left Lightning's stall. "Lightning tried to kick me," she said softly.

"Your trouble with Lightning is not just your problem," said Lulu. "It's a Pony Pal Problem."

Pam nodded.

As the three friends walked away from Lightning's stall, Pam looked over her shoulder. Her pony was still turned away from her.

"We saw your mother outside," said Lulu. "She asked us to set the table for dinner."

Pam stopped in her tracks. "You didn't tell her about Lightning, did you?" she asked.

"No," said Lulu. "But we really think you should."

"I don't want to tell her," said Pam. "I know Lightning better than she does."

"Let's have a Pony Pal meeting tonight,"

suggested Lulu. "Everybody have an idea ready to help Lightning."

"Okay," agreed Pam.

Jill ran from the house to meet the Pony Pals. "Splash was good for me," she shouted.

"Hey, that's great, Jill," said Lulu.

Jill walked between Anna and Pam. She looked up happily at Pam. "You made him be good," she said. "I love him. I love ponies best in the whole world."

"So do we," said Lulu.

"I groomed Splash after I rode him," Jill continued. "I put ribbons in his mane. He let me."

"That's great, Jill," said Lulu.

"Maybe your mom and dad will get you and Jack ponies of your own," said Lulu.

"I only want to ride Splash," said Jill. "I want Splash to be my very own pony."

"Splash has a great personality," said Anna.

Lightning is my very own pony, thought Pam. But now she won't even let me touch her.

Jill helped the Pony Pals set the big round kitchen table for dinner. She talked about Splash the whole time. As everyone else sat down to eat, Lulu went over to the kitchen counter. She wrote something on the memo pad, pulled the paper off the pad, and put it in her pocket.

Lulu has an idea about Lightning, thought Pam.

During dinner Mrs. Crandal told Dr. Crandal how beautifully Pam worked with Splash.

"Mommy, Mommy," interrupted Jill. "I want to ride Splash every day. Can I go for a trail ride with the Pony Pals?"

"Not yet," Mrs. Crandal answered. "Splash needs to be reminded of trail-riding manners before you ride him." She handed Pam the bowl of spaghetti. "Pam, will you give Splash a trail-riding lesson?"

"Please say yes, Pam," begged Jill. "Then I can go trail riding on him."

"Yes," answered Pam.

"Then can I trail ride Splash with the Pony Pals?" asked Jill.

"I want to go on a trail ride, too," said Jack. "Me and Daisy."

Jill pulled on Pam's arm. "Take us. Please."

"Ouch!" exclaimed Pam as she pulled her arm away from Jill.

Dr. Crandal looked concerned. "What's wrong with your arm?" he asked.

Pam and Anna exchanged a quick glance. Pam shifted in her seat. Her rear end hurt, too.

"Nothing," Pam told her father. "I just bumped it."

Pam wondered if she'd be able to work with Splash. Had she lost her ability to communicate with all ponies? Or just Lightning?

During kitchen cleanup, Anna sat back down at the table. She pulled out her sketchbook and made a drawing.

Anna must be drawing her idea about my problem with Lightning, thought Pam. Pam had an idea, too. She went over to the memo pad on the counter and quickly wrote it down. Her idea made her sad.

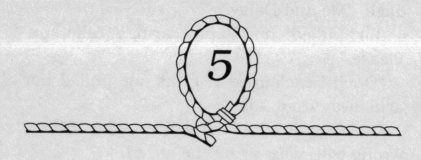

Three Ideas

The Pony Pals said good night to Pam's parents and the twins, and then went out to the barn office.

The three friends sat in a circle on their rolled-up sleeping bags. It was time for the Pony Pal meeting.

Pam began the meeting. "This meeting is about a very big problem," she said. "Lightning won't let me ride her. She even tried to kick me."

"What's your idea, Pam?" asked Lulu.

Pam handed Lulu her idea. Lulu read:

Lightning doesn't like me anymore.

"Why would Lightning stop liking you?" asked Anna.

"First, she was jealous because I rode Splash," began Pam. "Then, when she was hard to ride, I was mean to her. I pulled hard on the reins. I was angry and afraid, and she knew it." Pam swallowed to try to keep from crying. "Now she won't pay any attention to me at all. I can't communicate with her."

"She's not acting like herself with our ponies, either," said Anna. "She was mean to Snow White and she bit Acorn for no reason. Remember?"

Pam nodded.

"What's your idea, Anna?" asked Lulu.

Anna put her drawing in the middle of the circle. Pam and Lulu leaned forward and looked at it.

"My idea is that you've gotten too tall to ride Lightning," explained Anna.

"If a person is too big for a pony," said Lulu sadly, "it's harder to ride."

"You're the tallest Pony Pal," added Anna.

"But Lightning is tall for a pony," said Pam. "Besides, my mother measured us both last week. She said I'll be able to ride Lightning for a long time."

"I'm so glad I was wrong," said Anna. She gave Pam a friendly shove. "Aren't you glad I was wrong?"

The shove pushed Pam off her rolled-up sleeping bag. She hit the floor with her backside. "Ouch!" shouted Pam.

"Sorry," said Anna. "Did you hit your butt again?"

"And my arm," answered Pam angrily. "What are you so happy about, Anna? You had a bad idea and we still haven't solved the problem."

"I'm sorry I didn't have a better idea," snapped Anna. "I did my best. And I'm sorry you hurt your stupid butt."

Anna and Pam glared at each other.

Lulu put up her hands. "Everybody calm down," she said.

"Why are you angry at me?" asked Anna. "Lightning is the problem, not us."

"I'm sorry," said Pam quietly. "My arm and butt hurt from falling off Lightning. It's making me crabby."

"That's my idea," said Lulu.

"Your idea is that I'm crabby?" exclaimed Pam. "You think that's why Lightning is misbehaving?"

"No," said Lulu. She handed her idea to Pam. "Here, read it."

Pam read Lulu's idea out loud.

Lightning is misbehaving because something is physically wrong with her.

"Pam, you're acting crabby with us because your arm and butt hurt," explained Lulu. "Maybe Lightning is misbehaving because she's sick."

"But Lightning doesn't seem sick," said Pam. "She's finishing all her food. She doesn't have trouble breathing, and she hasn't been coughing."

"Maybe something is wrong that we don't know about," said Anna. "We should ask your father to give Lightning a checkup tomorrow."

"Okay," agreed Pam. "It's the only good idea we have."

Anna stood up. "I want to go see Lightning now," she said. "I'm worried about her."

"Let's spy on her and see how she acts when she's alone," added Lulu.

The girls tiptoed quietly to Lightning's stall.

They stopped where they could see Lightning, but Lightning couldn't see them. Fat Cat was sitting on the stall door watching Lightning, too.

Fat Cat jumped on Lightning's back. Lightning snorted, pinned back her ears, and shifted her weight. Fat Cat slid off Lightning's back.

The surprised cat meowed and scampered under the stall door.

Pam and Anna exchanged a glance. Lightning wasn't even being nice to her favorite cat. She didn't want anyone on her back.

Fat Cat rubbed against Pam's leg. Pam bent over and picked up the fluffy cat. "Poor Fat Cat," she said. "You don't know what's wrong with Lightning, either."

The girls walked up to the stall door.

"Hey, girl," said Pam softly.

Lightning ignored her.

"She only ate a little bit from her hay-rack," observed Anna.

Pam looked into the water bucket. "And she didn't drink very much of her water," she added.

A chill ran through Pam. Lightning was sick. But what was wrong? Would her father know?

"Let's go get my father now," said Pam.

The three girls ran to the house and went in through the kitchen door. Mrs. Crandal was sitting at the table drinking a cup of tea and reading the newspaper. "Sh-hh," she warned. "The twins just went to bed." She smiled at the girls. "Are you three looking for a nighttime snack?"

"We need to talk to Dad," said Pam. "Where is he?"

"He's in his study," Mrs. Crandal answered. Her smile disappeared. "What's happened?" she asked.

"It's Lightning," answered Pam. "Something is wrong with her."

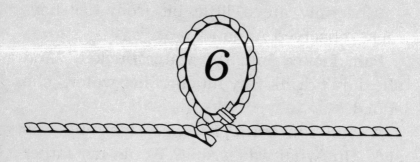

Blood Test

Mrs. Crandal and the Pony Pals went up to Dr. Crandal's study. Pam told her parents about her problems riding Lightning.

"Why didn't you tell us when you came home from your ride?" asked Pam's mother. "Or at dinner?"

"Because I thought it was my fault," mumbled Pam.

"But you're an excellent rider, honey," said Mrs. Crandal. "You and Lightning have a wonderful connection."

"Not anymore," said Pam.

Mrs. Crandal put an arm around Pam's shoulder.

"Don't hug her," Anna warned Mrs. Crandal. "Her arm is sore from falling off Lightning."

Pam's mother looked alarmed.

"I'm okay," Pam told her mother. "It's Lightning I'm worried about."

"I know," Mrs. Crandal said softly. "But let me look at your arm."

While Mrs. Crandal looked at Pam's bruised arm, Dr. Crandal put on his boots and jacket. Then they all headed out to the barn.

Dr. Crandal went into Lightning's stall. Everyone else watched from the barn aisle. Dr. Crandal looked into Lightning's eyes. "I hear you're not feeling so well, Lightning," he said. He took the pony's temperature. "No fever," he reported.

"I didn't think she had one," said Pam.

Dr. Crandal took out his stethoscope and listened to Lightning's lungs and heart. Next, he looked in Lightning's mouth and felt her glands. "Respiratory system checks out," he announced.

"I'm glad she doesn't have pneumonia," commented Lulu.

He ran his hands along Lightning's back and legs. "I'm checking her muscles and joints," he explained. As Dr. Crandal felt Lightning's joints, she tried to move away from him.

"Why doesn't she want you to do that, Dad?" asked Pam.

"There's swelling," he answered. "And she has some sore muscles and joints."

"Why are her muscles sore?" asked Anna. "She didn't fall."

"I don't know why," Dr. Crandal answered. He took a needle and syringe out of his medical bag. "I'll take a blood sample and send it to the lab. Maybe that will tell us what's wrong."

Pam watched her father draw blood from a vein in Lightning's neck. She didn't mind needles and shots. She wanted to be a veterinarian herself someday. Lulu watched, too, but Anna covered her eyes.

Dr. Crandal put the sample in his bag and asked Pam to lead Lightning up and down the aisle. "I want to see her walk," he explained.

Pam led Lightning out of the stall and down the aisle.

"She's limping a little on her front right leg," Mrs. Crandal observed.

Pam noticed the limp, too. "She wasn't doing that before," she said. "I would have noticed."

"Do you think Lightning has Lyme?" Mrs. Crandal asked Dr. Crandal.

"It's a possibility," he answered.

"What's Lyme?" asked Anna.

"Lyme disease is what you get when a tick bites you," Pam explained.

"I know what a tick is," said Anna. "They have lots of short legs."

"A tiny black tick can give you Lyme disease," explained Lulu. "Mr. Olson had Lyme disease, remember?"

"He was really tired and said he ached all over," remembered Anna. "But he's okay now."

"How could Lightning have Lyme disease?" Pam asked her father. "There aren't any ticks around now. It's winter and everything is frozen."

"There's no tall grass," added Lulu. "That's where people and animals get ticks."

"She could have been bitten months ago," he answered. "Some people and animals don't get sick right away."

Pam led Lightning back into her stall. She looked into her pony's sad eyes and felt very sad herself. Lightning dropped her head and looked at the ground.

"Will she get sicker?" asked Anna.

"What can we do to make her better?" added Pam.

"Is Lyme curable, Dr. Crandal?" asked Lulu.

Dr. Crandal put up his hands. "Whoa," he said. "Slow down. First, we have to send out the blood and find out if it *is* Lyme."

"And if it is?" asked Pam.

"We give her antibiotics," answered Dr. Crandal. "And we wait and see."

Mrs. Crandal brushed a strand of hair off Pam's face. "Your pony will have the best care, honey," she said. "You know that."

Tears filled Pam's eyes. "But you can't promise me she'll get better," she said.

"We don't even know if she has Lyme," Mrs. Crandal reminded Pam.

"Dad, when will the test come back?" asked Pam.

Dr. Crandal snapped his medical bag shut. "I'll send her blood out first thing tomorrow," he said. "The earliest we'll have results is late tomorrow afternoon."

"What can we do for her while we wait?" asked Pam.

"Let her rest as much as she wants," he answered. "The best thing you can do is to go to bed and stop worrying."

"I can't stop worrying, Dad," said Pam.

Dr. Crandal put an arm around his daughter and gave her a squeeze. "I know, honey," he said. Pam's arm hurt when her father hugged her. But she didn't care. She just wanted her pony to be better.

Pam's mother and father went back to the house and the Pony Pals went to the barn office.

"Let's look up Lyme disease on the Internet," suggested Lulu.

"Good idea," agreed Anna.

Pam turned on the computer and went online. She searched for a medical guide about ponies and horses. When she found the site, Pam typed in LYME DISEASE and pressed ENTER. An article about Lyme disease came up on the screen. The three girls huddled around the computer to read.

"Lyme disease isn't catching," commented Lulu. "The only way you can get it is from a tick."

"So the other ponies can't catch it from Lightning," concluded Anna. "I was worried about that."

"And we won't catch it from her, either," added Lulu.

"Look here," said Pam, pointing to the screen. "Sore muscles and joints are a symptom."

51

"That's why Lightning didn't want you to ride her," concluded Anna. "Because of her sore muscles."

"She was in pain," added Pam sadly.

"It says here antibiotics are the only treatment," said Lulu. *"Sometimes the first antibiotic doesn't work and a second round of antibiotics is prescribed."* Lulu didn't read the last two sentences of the article.

Pam stared at the screen and read them to herself. *In some cases,* she read, *the pony or horse is not cured and could have Lyme for the rest of its life. Such an animal may suffer various muscular, joint, and neurological symptoms.*

"Lightning might not even have Lyme disease," Lulu said as she closed the file.

"Lightning will be okay," said Anna. "We'll take good care of her."

Pam knew that taking good care of her pony might not be enough. If Lightning had Lyme disease, she might never get better. Pam felt confused, tired, and very frightened.

"I'm going to say good night to Lightning," she told her friends.

Anna and Lulu nodded. They understood that Pam needed to be alone with her pony.

Lightning was sleeping standing up. I won't wake her, Pam thought. She needs her rest.

Pam looked out through the barn window. The night sky was cloudy. She looked until she spotted one small star.

"Star light, star bright," she whispered, "the first star I see tonight. I wish I may, I wish I might have the wish I wish tonight. Please let my pony, Lightning, be all right."

Waiting

Pam was the first Pony Pal to wake up the next morning. She crawled out of her sleeping bag and put on her boots.

Lulu rolled over and opened her eyes. "Where are you going?" she asked sleepily.

"To check on Lightning," answered Pam. "I'll give her some oats."

"I'll go with you," said Lulu.

Anna sat up, stretched her arms, and yawned. "Me, too," she said.

When the girls reached the stall, Lightning was awake.

"Hey, girl, how are you today?" asked Pam.

"Hi, Lightning," said Anna.

Lightning moved restlessly around the stall, but she didn't look at the girls.

"I think she's in pain," observed Pam sadly. "That's why she's moving around like that."

Lightning ate some oats and drank a little water.

"I'm going to walk her in the aisle," Pam told her friends. "I want to see if she's still limping."

"We'll clean her stall while you do that," offered Lulu.

"Thanks," said Pam. She led Lightning into the aisle. Lightning wasn't limping on her front right leg anymore. Now the sick pony was favoring her left back leg.

"A different leg is sore," Pam told her friends.

"Soreness can go to different parts of the body," said Lulu. "I read that in the article about Lyme disease."

"Lulu's right," a male voice said. Pam

looked up. Her father had come into the barn. He ran his hand softly over Lightning's neck. "But we won't be sure it's Lyme disease until we get the lab report."

"How will you get the lab report, Dad?" asked Pam. "Do they e-mail it to you?"

"The lab will fax it," her father replied. "I have barn calls this afternoon. I'll look for it when I get back."

Pam and Anna exchanged a glance. They knew where the fax machine was in the office. They could check for the fax themselves.

After breakfast, Jill followed the Pony Pals out to the barn. She helped them roll up their sleeping bags. While the Pony Pals fed Snow White and Acorn, Jill fed Splash. When Lulu and Anna brought their ponies' saddles out to the paddock, Jill carried the bridles for them.

"Splash and me want to do everything like the Pony Pals," she said.

Anna and Pam exchanged a glance. Pam

rolled her eyes. Would Jill want to tag along with them all the time?

"Anna and Lulu have to go home now," Pam told Jill.

"How come?" asked Jill.

"I'm going out to brunch with my grandmother," answered Lulu. "It's her birthday."

"And I have to see my tutor," said Anna as she placed the saddle on Acorn's back. "She's going to help me with my book report."

"The book report!" gasped Lulu. "I forgot all about it. I'll have to write it after lunch."

Pam slipped the bridle on Acorn's head. "I've only read about half of my book," said Pam. "I'll finish reading it while I'm watching Lightning."

Mrs. Crandal joined the group at the paddock. "Are you two going home on Pony Pal Trail?" she asked Anna and Lulu.

"Yes," answered Lulu.

Pony Pal Trail was a mile-and-a-half trail through the woods. It connected the Crandals' property with Snow White and Acorn's paddock. It was a perfect shortcut for the Pony Pals.

"Pam, why don't you ride Splash on Pony Pal Trail with Anna and Lulu," suggested Mrs. Crandal. "He needs to practice his trail-riding manners."

Jill clapped her hands excitedly. "If Splash has manners, I can take him on a trail ride," she exclaimed.

"I can't do it today, Mom," said Pam.

Jill pulled on Pam's hand. "Please ride him, please."

"I'm staying with Lightning all day," Pam told her.

"I'll keep an eye on Lightning for you," Mrs. Crandal promised.

"Me, too," added Jill.

"I don't want to leave Lightning today," insisted Pam. "We don't even know what's wrong with her yet. I'll ride Splash on the trail another time."

"I can't trail ride him until you do it," said Jill sadly.

"Lightning is sick," said Pam sharply. "That's more important."

"I know," mumbled Jill.

Lulu and Anna mounted their ponies.

"Call us as soon as you know the results of Lightning's blood test," said Lulu.

"Or if she gets worse," added Anna sadly.

"I will," promised Pam.

As Lulu and Anna rode away, Pam headed back to the barn. Jill skipped along beside her. "I want to take care of Lightning, too," she said.

"There isn't anything you can do," Pam told her.

"What are you going to do?" asked Jill.

"Watch her," said Pam.

Jill followed her sister into the barn.

"Will you do something for me, Jill?" Pam asked.

"Okay," agreed Jill.

"Go to the house and get my book out of my school backpack," instructed Pam. "It's on my desk."

While Jill was gone, Pam put a sawhorse

in front of the stall door. She sat on the sawhorse and watched Lightning. Jill came back with the book and Pam silently began to read. At the end of every page, she checked on Lightning.

Jill sat next to Pam. She watched Lightning, too. And Pam.

"Why are you staring at me?" Pam asked her.

"Will you ride Splash tomorrow?" asked Jill.

"I don't know," said Pam impatiently. "Jill, please go find something else to do. Why don't you draw? Anna says you're a good artist. I think you are, too. You can draw great ponies."

Jill jumped down from the sawhorse. "Okay," she said cheerfully. "I'll come back when I finish."

"Do lots of pictures," Pam called after her.

Pam hoped that Jill would be busy for a long time. She wanted to be alone with Lightning.

After Jill left, Pam read out loud to Lightning. When she looked up at the end of the page, Lightning was asleep.

Pam went back to silent reading.

Lightning woke up and nickered as if to say, "Why'd you stop reading to me?" She shifted her weight from side to side.

Pam read out loud again. Lightning fell back to sleep.

A warm feeling came over Pam. There *was* something she could do for her pony. If she read out loud, Lightning would rest.

At lunchtime, Mrs. Crandal brought Pam a sandwich and juice. "I thought you might like to eat out here," she said.

"Thanks," said Pam.

Pam stopped reading to eat. When Lightning woke up, Pam gave her a carrot. Lightning ate the carrot and drank some water, but she didn't nibble at the hay in her hayrack.

After lunch, Pam went back to reading out loud and Lightning went back to resting.

At one o'clock, Pam left the barn and ran

over to her father's animal clinic. The fax machine was behind the desk. Pam saw that one fax transmittal had come in. HEALTHY BRAND VITAMINS KEEP HORSES HEALTHY was written in a banner across the top.

It wasn't Lightning's blood test results. It was an advertisement for vitamins.

For the next hour, Pam worked on her book report while Lightning rested. But it was difficult for Pam to concentrate. She was too worried about her pony.

At two o'clock, Pam checked the fax machine again. Four lab reports had been transmitted. None of them was about Lightning.

N = Not at All

At four o'clock, Pam went back to her father's office. There were no new faxes. Pam felt discouraged. Would she have to wait until the next day to find out if Lightning had Lyme disease?

As Pam was leaving the office, the fax phone rang. She ran back to the fax machine and watched the fax come out. She picked it up and read:

National Animal Laboratory

PATIENT: Lightning.

OWNER: Pam Crandal.

Pam's heart began to beat fast as she quickly scanned the page and read: *The patient has acute Lyme disease*. Pam finally knew for sure what was wrong with Lightning. Now they could begin treatment. She needed her father.

Pam went to the back of the animal clinic. Her father's assistant, Joe, was sweeping the examining-room floor.

"Joe, when's my dad getting back?" Pam asked.

"Don't know," Joe answered. "He had a lot of barn visits. Anything I can do for you?"

Pam held out the paper. "This just came in," she said. "Lightning has Lyme disease."

Joe took the paper and looked it over. "Your dad's at the Olsons' farm," he said. "I'll call and tell him. He'd want to know right away." Joe looked kindly at Pam. "Sorry about Lightning, Pam."

Pam thanked Joe and left the clinic. She remembered that her mother and the twins had gone grocery shopping. Pam ran back to the barn and phoned Anna. "Lightning has Lyme," she blurted out.

"I'll tell Lulu," said Anna. "We'll be right there."

Pam went back to Lightning. She kissed her pony on the cheek. Lightning didn't nod or snuggle Pam as she usually did.

"I know you're not mad at me, Lightning," said Pam. "You're sick with Lyme disease. We're going to do everything we can to make you better. I promise."

Half an hour later, Dr. Crandal was in Lightning's stall with Pam.

"We'll start the antibiotic treatment right away," he said as he filled a syringe. Pam held Lightning's head while Dr. Crandal gave the pony the antibiotic shot in the neck.

Anna and Lulu arrived a few minutes later.

"How long before she's better, Dr. Crandal?" asked Lulu.

"If she hasn't improved in a week," he answered, "I'll try a different antibiotic."

"And if the second antibiotic doesn't work?" asked Pam.

"Let's take it one week at a time, honey," answered Dr. Crandal.

Pam knew that if the second antibiotic didn't work her father wouldn't give up. He would do all he could to cure Lightning. She also knew that some ponies never recovered from Lyme disease.

"I'm not going to school this week," Pam told her father. "I have to stay with Lightning."

"Me, too," said Anna. "I'll help."

"You'll use any excuse to play hooky, Anna Harley," Dr. Crandal teased.

"But I want to help Lightning," protested Anna.

Dr. Crandal put a hand on Anna's shoulder. "I know," he said. He turned to Pam. "If I thought it would make a difference, I'd let you miss school, Pam. But it won't."

"She's my pony," Pam protested. "And she's so sick, Dad."

"You can take care of her before school, like always," he said. "Your mother will look in on her during the day. When you come home from school, I'll give her the daily shot."

"Dr. Crandal, how can we tell if Lightning is getting better?" asked Anna.

"There are a few things you can look for," he answered.

Pam took out her little notebook and wrote down what her father said.

After Dr. Crandal left the barn, the Pony Pals had an emergency Pony Pal meeting. They all read Pam's notes. Then they made a chart for tracking Lightning's progress during the week. "I'll make a good copy later and tape it to the stall door," Pam promised.

Next, they made a schedule for staying with Lightning.

"I have tutoring on Monday and Wednesday after school," Anna reminded Pam.

"And I have my piano lesson on Tuesday," remembered Lulu.

Pam wrote up a schedule.

	Before School	**After School**
Monday	Pam	Pam and Lulu
Tuesday	Pam	Pam and Anna
Wednesday	Pam	Pam and Lula
Thursday	Pam	Pam and Anna
Friday	Pam	Pam, Anna, and Lulu

When she finished the schedule, Pam looked out the window. "It will be dark soon," she told Anna and Lulu. "You'd better go."

A few minutes later, Pam watched her friends ride toward Pony Pal Trail. She wondered when she would ride her pony again. Tears rolled down her cheeks. I might never ride Lightning again, she thought.

That night, after dinner, Pam made a good copy of the progress report chart.

It was time for bed, but first Pam wanted to check on Lightning. She put on her boots and jacket and went out to the barn. After she taped the progress report chart to the stall door, she checked the hayrack. Lightning hadn't eaten any of the fresh hay.

PROGRESS REPORT ON LIGHTNING
HOW IS HER APPETITE?
    1 = very poor appetite
    2 = poor appetite
    3 = improved appetite
    4 = normal appetite

IS SHE LAME?
 Y = yes / N = no

IS SHE FRIENDLY?
Y = yes / AL = a little / N = not at all

EYES
UH = unhappy / AC = almost clear /
C = clear and calm

OTHER OBSERVATIONS AND COMMENTS:

Next to "How is her appetite?" on the progress chart, Pam wrote a 1 for very poor appetite.

Pam walked Lightning in the barn aisle.

She was favoring her front right leg. Next to "Is she lame?" Pam wrote Y for yes.

She scratched Lightning's upside-down heart marking. Usually, Lightning liked to have her forehead scratched. But now she didn't care. The sick pony ignored Pam.

Next to "Is she friendly?" Pam wrote N for not at all. She looked into Lightning's eyes. They were very unhappy. So Pam wrote UH next to Eyes.

Under "Other observations and comments" Pam wrote: "I hope you are better tomorrow, Lightning."

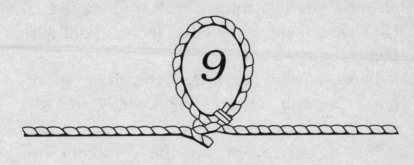

Progress Report

MONDAY

Early the next morning, Pam fed Lightning and cleaned out her stall. Next, she answered the questions on the progress report. Lightning's appetite, lameness, friendliness, and eyes were 1–Y–N–UH. There was no progress.

Pam didn't want to leave her sick pony, but she had to go to school.

That afternoon, Lulu went home with Pam. When they got off the school bus, they ran straight to the barn. Lightning was the same as in the morning. The two girls cleaned out Lightning's stall and waited for Dr. Crandal. An hour later, Dr. Crandal gave Lightning her shot.

Pam showed her father the progress report. "Lightning hasn't improved, Dad," she said.

"She's only been on the antibiotic for twenty-four hours," he reminded Pam. "Be patient and let her rest."

I can't be patient, thought Pam. I'm too scared that Lightning won't get better. What if she's sick for the rest of her life? I might never be able to ride her again. It would be the end of all the good riding times with my pony.

After Lulu left, Pam read her history homework to Lightning. The sick pony lowered her head and closed her eyes.

While Pam was reading, Jill climbed up on the sawhorse beside her. Pam ignored her sister and continued reading.

"I fed Splash," announced Jill.

"Good for you," said Pam. She continued to read out loud.

"Is Lightning better?" asked Jill.

"No," answered Pam. "Not yet."

"I'm glad Splash isn't sick," said Jill.

Pam knew what Jill would say next.

"When are you going — " began Jill.

Pam turned to her. "I'm *not* trail riding Splash for you today," she said firmly. "I don't know when I can do it. *Don't ask me again!*"

"I wasn't going to ask you to ride Splash," said Jill huffily. She jumped down from the sawhorse. "I was going to ask you something else."

"What?" Pam asked. "What were you going to ask me?"

"When are you going — " Jill hesitated. "When are you going — to set the table for dinner?"

"Jill, you just made that up!" exclaimed Pam. "You were going to ask me to ride Splash."

"Who cares?" shouted Jill as she ran from the barn.

Lightning shifted uncomfortably from side to side.

"Sorry, Lightning," said Pam.

Pam continued reading to Lightning, but she wasn't thinking about history. She was thinking about how she had treated Jill. First I was angry at my pony, she thought. Then I was grumpy with my best friends. Now I'm being mean to my little sister. I'm turning into a not-very-nice person.

At six o'clock, Pam closed her book and hopped off the sawhorse. It was time to go in and set the table. She kissed Lightning on her upside-down heart marking. Lightning's eyes looked dull to Pam. Her pony was still very sick. "I'll come back after dinner," she promised.

Pam walked slowly to the house and into the kitchen. She couldn't stop worrying about Lightning. Her mother looked up from making salad and smiled at her. "Someone has a surprise for you," she said.

Pam looked around the room. The table was already set. "Thanks, Mom," she said.

"I didn't do it," said her mother. "Jill did. And she made you something."

There was a folded piece of paper on Pam's plate. Pam's name was written in big print on the outside. "Jill wants me to trail ride Splash for her," Pam told her mother. She pulled off the tape and looked at what Jill had made.

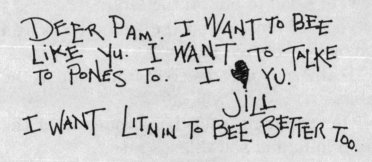

DEER PAM. I WANT TO BEE
LIKE Yu. I WANT TO TALKE
TO PONES TO. I ♥ YU.
                          JILL
I WANT LITNIN TO BEE BETTER TOO.

Pam studied the cute drawing. She was sorry she'd been so grumpy with her little sister.

"Did she ask you to trail ride Splash?" asked her mother.

"Not really," answered Pam as she refolded the letter. "Are you using him for lessons tomorrow afternoon, Mom?"

"I'll be finished with him by three," answered Mrs. Crandal. She handed Pam a big bowl of salad to put on the table.

"I'll take him out on the trail after school tomorrow," offered Pam.

"Yeah!" a voice cheered from under the table.

Pam squatted, pulled up the side of the tablecloth, and saw Jill.

"You sneak, Jill Crandal," said Pam as she pulled out her sister. Pam wiggled her fingers over Jill's belly. "The tickle-torture machine is going to get you for that," she warned.

Jill giggled and squirmed as Pam tickled her.

I'll trail ride Splash for Jill, thought Pam.

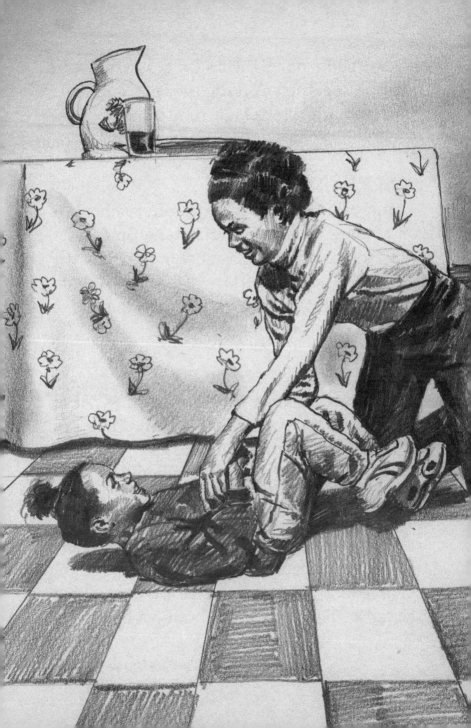

And as soon as Lightning's better we can trail ride together. A dark thought suddenly crossed Pam's mind. Lightning might not get better.

TUESDAY

Anna went home with Pam after school. It was raining, so she couldn't take Splash for a trail ride. Lightning was the same as the day before and the day before that. Pam swallowed hard to keep from crying when she filled out the progress report.

WEDNESDAY

The day was very cold, but sunny. After school, Lulu went home with Pam. They ran from the school bus to the barn.

Lightning didn't look up when the girls came to her stall.

Pam checked her pony's eyes. Lightning still looked unhappy. She was also still lame and not very friendly.

"I'm going to take Splash out now," Pam told Lulu. "I'll be back in about an hour."

"Don't worry about Lightning," said Lulu. "I'm here. And she won't see you riding Splash."

Pam left the barn. Lightning is too sick with Lyme to care if I ride another pony, she thought. And she may never recover.

Me, Too

Mrs. Crandal, Jill, and Splash were waiting for Pam near the riding ring.

Jill ran her fingers through Splash's mane. "I brushed him and told him to be good," she reported.

"Who's riding with you?" Mrs. Crandal asked Pam. "You can't teach Splash trail-riding manners if he's the only pony."

"Anna and Acorn are meeting us on the trail," answered Pam as she mounted Splash. She said good-bye to her mother and

sister and rode across the field to the beginning of Pony Pal Trail.

Pam often helped her mother with the
school ponies. She'd ridden them a lot and
had fun doing it. But riding Splash today
made her sad. It reminded her that she
might never ride Lightning again.

I have to concentrate on Splash, Pam told
herself. Jill loves him very much. I want her
to be able to ride him.

On the first part of the trail, Pam kept
Splash to a walk. She was firm with him and
he followed her commands. "Good pony," she
said encouragingly.

Anna and Acorn were waiting at the three
birch trees.

"You lead," Pam told Anna. "I have to
make sure Splash stays in line."

Anna trotted Acorn along a wide, straight
section of the trail. Splash rushed to pass
Acorn.

"Whoa," said Pam as she reined him in.

Anna and Pam rode the ponies over the

same section of trail three times. Each time Acorn led. Each time Splash tried to over-take Acorn. The fourth time Splash stayed in line.

After forty-five minutes, the two riders pulled up beside each other.

"I have to go back," Anna told Pam, "or I'll be late for my tutor."

"Thanks for helping," said Pam.

"Do you think Jill can trail ride Splash now?" asked Anna.

"I should work with him one more time," answered Pam. "But I can take him out alone the next time."

THURSDAY

It was Anna's turn to help Pam with Light-ning after school. When the two friends reached the barn, Anna took a good look at Lightning. "She looks better than the last time I saw her," she said.

Suddenly, Lightning turned and whinnied softly at Pam. Tears of happiness sprung to Pam's eyes. Maybe the antibiotic was working. Maybe Lightning *was* getting better.

Pam hooked the lead rope to Lightning's halter and led her into the aisle. She walked Lightning up and down.

"She's still limping a little," observed Anna. "But not as much as before."

The girls filled in the progress report. Lightning had improved in every category.

When Jill came into the barn to check on Lightning, Pam told her the good news.

"Will you ride Splash again today?" asked Jill.

"Sure," agreed Pam. "But you have to help me saddle him up. Okay?"

"Okay!" shouted Jill. "Let's go." Jill was already running out of the barn.

"I'll stay with Lightning," said Anna with a laugh.

A few minutes later, Pam rode Splash onto Pony Pal Trail. Pam remembered all the times she'd ridden Lightning on the familiar trail. I hope the next pony I ride is Lightning, Pam thought. I miss riding my pony so much.

FRIDAY

The Pony Pals met in front of the school.

"How's Lightning?" Anna and Lulu asked in unison.

"She wasn't lame at all this morning," reported Pam. "My dad said I can put her out in the paddock this afternoon."

The Pony Pals hit high fives and cheered.

Pam didn't mind being in school on Friday. While she was doing her schoolwork, Lightning was getting better. The antibiotic was working.

During math, Anna passed Pam a note. It was from Lulu. Pam put the note in her opened math book and read it.

Anna: After school we should ride SW and A to Pam's. Lightning must miss them.

P.S. Pass this note to Pam.

Lulu.

Good idea! I can do it.
Anna

Pam looked up. The Pony Pals exchanged a glance. Pam nodded. She wanted Lightning to see her friends. She just hoped that her pony would be nice to Acorn and Snow White. She hoped that Lightning would be back to normal.

When Pam arrived home she ran right to the barn. She couldn't wait to see Lightning. "Hey, girl," she called out.

Lightning whinnied back a cheerful hello. Pam gave her pony some oats and cleaned out her stall. She whistled the whole time. Her pony was really getting better.

Pam led Lightning outside. Lightning sniffed the air, looked around, and whinnied. She was happy to be outdoors. Pam let her loose in the paddock and watched. Lightning didn't run but walked slowly around the paddock. At least she's not limping, thought Pam. She jumped up on the fence and waited for her friends.

A half hour later, Anna and Lulu came off Pony Pal Trail and cantered toward the paddock. Lightning looked up. When the riders halted in front of the fence, Acorn snorted at Lightning. He seemed to be saying, "Are you my friend, or what?"

Lightning walked over to the fence. She lowered her head and Acorn sniffed her face. Lightning whinnied softly.

Snow White pushed her body against Acorn. She wanted to sniff faces with Lightning, too.

"That's so beautiful," said Anna. "They're great friends." The three Pony Pals smiled at one another. Everything was going to be okay.

"Here come the twins and your mother," announced Lulu. Jack and Jill ran up to the Pony Pals and their ponies. Mrs. Crandal came up behind them.

"Can we go trail riding with you?" Jack asked the Pony Pals.

"Mom said we could if you say yes," added Jill.

"Yes," said Lulu and Anna in unison.

The twins hit high fives.

Mrs. Crandal gently rubbed Lightning's

neck. "Lightning is a lot better today," she said.

"But not better enough to ride," Pam told her.

"I know," said her mother. "But your father said she's recovering nicely." She put an arm around Pam's shoulder and gave her a little squeeze. "I'm so glad."

"Me, too, Mom," agreed Pam.

"Are you going trail riding, Pam?" Jill asked.

"I can't ride Lightning yet," explained Pam.

"You can take Sterling out on the trail," her mother offered.

"You'd let Pam ride *your* horse?!" exclaimed Jill.

"She's tall enough to ride him," said Mrs. Crandal. "I think she'd have a great ride on Sterling."

"No, thanks, Mom," said Pam. "You ride with them." She scratched Lightning's upside-down heart. "I want to stay with my pony."

Pam helped the twins and her mother saddle up Splash, Daisy, and Sterling. Then she went into the paddock with Lightning. They watched the parade of ponies, horse, and their riders going across the field to Pony Pal Trail.

Lightning nudged Pam to get her attention. She turned to her pony. "We'll go trail riding soon," she said.

Lightning rested her muzzle on Pam's shoulder. Just like always.

Pam leaned her head against her pony's neck. "I love you, too," she said.

Pony Pals

Be a Pony Pal®!

Available wherever you buy books, or use this order form.

Send orders to Scholastic Inc., P.O. Box 7500, Jefferson City, MO 65102

Please send me the books I have checked above. I am enclosing $_____ (please add $2.00 to cover shipping and handling). Send check or money order — no cash or C.O.D.s please.

Please allow four to six weeks for delivery. Offer good in the U.S.A. only. Sorry, mail orders are not available to residents of Canada. Prices subject to change.

Name_____ Birth Date ____/____/____

First   Last   M   D   Y

Address_____

City_____ State_____ Zip_____

Telephone (   ) _____ ☐ Boy   ☐ Girl

Where did you buy this book?   ☐ Bookstore   ☐ Book Fair   ☐ Book Club   ☐ Other   PP1101